It wasn't long before they met a man with a barrow full of straw.

"I could build a very good house with that straw," said the first little pig. He bought the lot.

The first little pig worked hard. By supper time, he had built himself a very snug little house.

Suddenly, there was a knock at the door. It was the Big, Bad Wolf!

"Little pig, little pig, let me come in!" called the wolf.

"No, no, by the hair on my chinny chin chin, I will *not* let you in!" said the first little pig.

"Then I'll huff and I'll puff and I'll blow your house down!" growled the wolf.

The Big, Bad Wolf took a deep breath and he blew the house down!

Meanwhile, the second and third little pigs walked on down the winding road. Soon they met a man with a load of sticks.

"I could make myself a very good house with those sticks," said the second little pig. He waved goodbye to his sister. Before long, he had built a wooden house.

Suddenly, there came a knock at the
door. It was the first little pig!
"Let me in!" he cried. "The Big, Bad
Wolf is close behind me!"

"Little pigs, little pigs, let me come in!"
growled the wolf.

"No, no, by the hair on our chinny chin chins," replied the two little
pigs, "we will *not* let you in!"

"Then I'll huff and I'll puff and I'll blow your house down!"

The Big, Bad Wolf took a deep breath. He *huffed* …

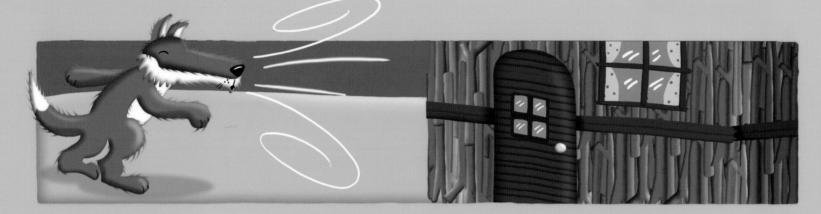

and he *puffed* …

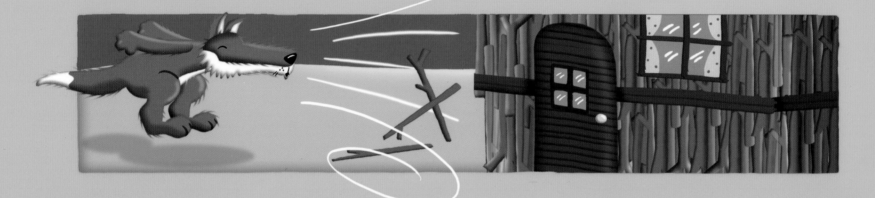

and he blew the house down!

★ ★ ★ ★ ★ ★ ★ ★ ★ ★ ★

Seeing that the Big, Bad Wolf was too puffed out to run, the two little pigs scuttled off to find their sister. She had met a man with a cart full of bricks. Very quickly, she had built a beautiful house.

Suddenly, there came a hammering at her door. "Let us in, let us in!" cried her brothers. "The Big, Bad Wolf is on his way!"

It wasn't long before they heard the wolf outside. "Little pigs, little pigs, let me come in!"

"No, no, by the hair on our chinny chin chins," chorused the three little pigs, "we will *not* let you in!"

"Then I'll huff and I'll puff and I'll blow your house down!" fumed the wolf.

So he *huffed* and he *puffed*. The little brick house stood strong and true.